OOPS! Excuse Me Please!

And Other Mannerly Tales

by Bob McGrath

Illustrations by Tammie Lyon

BARRON'S

All inquiries should be addressed to:
Barron's Educational Series, Inc.
250 Wireless Boulevard
Hauppauge, New York 11788

International Standard Book No. 0-7641-5083-9

Library of Congress Catalog Card No. 97-45015

Library of Congress Cataloging-in-Publication Data

McGrath, Bob, 1932-
    Oops! Excuse me please! : and other mannerly tales / by Bob
McGrath ; illustrations by Tammie Lyon.
        p.   cm.
    Summary: A collection of twenty-eight vignettes illustrating good
manners, covering such topics as proper etiquette, following the Golden
Rule, and memorizing correct phrases.
    ISBN 0-7641-5083-9
    1. Etiquette for children and teenagers. [1. Etiquette.]
I. Lyon, Tammie, ill. II. Title.
BJ1857.C5M14   1998
359.1'22—dc21
                                        97-45015
                                           CIP
                                           AC

Printed in Hong Kong/China
9 8 7 6 5 4

A Note to Parents

Researching this book turned out to be a lively and complicated endeavor for me. Everyone has their own opinion about what constitutes good manners. It seems that good manners can mean anything from being considerate to using proper etiquette, from following the golden rule, to memorizing a correct phrase. The manners chosen for this book include many of the ideas that people have suggested. The episodes have come from my wife's and my own experiences with our five children and five grandchildren and from the experiences of our neighbors and friends.

This is what we learned from reading other books already out there on the subject: Good manners make life run more smoothly. Good manners make other people feel good. Good manners help you to be a nice person. We agree with all of this. We also agree that good manners based on caring and consideration are a sign of maturity in a person.

In keeping with our views about teaching, a philosophy influenced by twenty-nine years on *Sesame Street,* we have tried to include a good amount of humor in this book. As you read to your child we hope that you will point out in each episode what is happening and why it's happening. You are your child's first and best teacher. Growing up with good manners can be a natural process when it includes everyone in the family.

Bob McGrath

No one is swinging because no one is taking turns.

Shelly says, "Hey, everybody! Taking turns works!"

Carla's mom and the saleslady are
both proud of her good manners.

Dick and Edmund forget to bring
their manners to the movies.

John Luis says, "Better not point, Nicky.
It makes people feel uncomfortable."

When Elizabeth gave a "little push,"
she made a big mistake.

Whispering secrets make Yasuko feel left out.

When Charlie uses a bad word,
he doesn't sound very nice.

Olivia is wondering why no
one can understand her.

Even the dog can't look at Jane's table manners.

Jill is thrilled she remembered
to put her napkin on her lap.

Nina should have said, "Please pass the pickles."

Ardash never forgets to say,
"May I please be excused?"

Rosita helps after dinner and always gets a smile.

Uh, oh! Russell's dad is ordering a peanut
butter and jelly pizza with ketchup
because everyone is interrupting him.

Patrick knows why kids should not
run in restaurants.

It's hard for Dorthea to leave
her favorite TV show,...

...but when her grandmother visits, she jumps right up and says, "Hi, Granny. It's great to see you."

Miles plays with quiet stuff
when his dad is snoozing.

Paul tries very hard to keep a sunny
attitude after Sean messes up his picture.

Luke knows it's a big help to
hold the door for his dad.

When Cheyenne answers the phone she says, "Hello. This is the Orman house."

When Amy's uncle says, "You're looking great!" Amy says, "Thank you."

When Eileen makes a funny noise
she says, "Oops! Excuse me."

Roger says, "No, thank you, Mrs. Spinny.
I don't care for asparagus tonight."

Walter says, "Excuse me please."

Will is proud of his first "Thank you" note.

Ian remembers to ask, "May
I ride your rocking horse?"

Joey always remembers to use a
tissue when he blows his nose.

Teddy is disappointed with Jenny's gift, but he
doesn't forget to say, "Thank you."

Even though Abby lost the race,

she knows that a good sport always says,
"Congratulations!"